Bike Daredevils

Felice Arena and Phil Kettle

illustrated by
David Cox

First published 2003 by
MACMILLAN EDUCATION AUSTRALIA PTY LTD
627 Chapel Street, South Yarra, Australia 3141

This edition first published in the United States of America
in 2004 by MONDO Publishing.

For information contact:
MONDO Publishing
980 Avenue of the Americas
New York, NY 10018

Visit our web site at http://www.mondopub.com

04 05 06 07 08 09   9 8 7 6 5 4 3 2 1

ISBN 1-59336-371-0 (PB)

Library of Congress Cataloging-in-Publication Data

Arena, Felice, 1968-
   Bike daredevils / Felice Arena and Phil Kettle ; illustrated by David Cox.
   p. cm. -- (Boyz rule!)
   Summary: When Con and Josh go cycling together, they experiment with
   various stunts.
   Includes related miscellanea as well as questions to test the reader's
   comprehension.
   ISBN: 1-59336-371-0 (pbk.)
   [1. Bicycles and bicycling--Fiction.] I. Kettle, Phil, 1955- II. Cox, David,
   1933 - ill. III. Title.

PZ7.A6825Bi 2004
[E]--dc22

                                                                2004047629

Project Management by Limelight Press Pty Ltd
Cover and text design by Lore Foye
Illustrations by David Cox

Printed in Hong Kong

Contents

Josh *Con*

CHAPTER 1

A Balancing Act

In a quiet suburban street, best friends Josh and Con are casually riding their bikes around in circles on the grass in front of Con's house.

Josh "What gear are you in?"

Con "Fourth. You?"

Josh "First. Can you balance when your bike's not moving?"

Con "Yeah. Can you?"

Josh "Yeah, course!"

Con "How long can you do it for?"

Josh "Don't know—probably about two minutes."

Con "No way! That's pretty long."

Josh "No, it's not. Look, I'll show ya! You time me."

Con "I haven't got a watch."

Josh "Me neither. Just time me by saying 'one Mississippi, two Mississippi...'"

Con "What?"

Josh "When you say 'one Mississippi,' it's about one second."

Con "Oh, like 'one monkey-kneebone, two monkey-kneebone...'"

Josh "Yeah—like that."

Con "Okay. One Mississippi, two Missi..."

Josh "Not yet! Wait! Start counting when I say I'm ready."

Josh stops pedaling his bike and gently squeezes his brakes until he rolls to a stop. He stands up out of his seat, swaying from side to side, struggling to keep upright.

Josh "Now!"

Con "One Mississippi, two Mississippi, three Mississippi, four monkey-kneebone, five monkey-kneebone…"

Josh suddenly loses his balance and begins to fall.

CHAPTER 2

And for My Next Trick...

Josh sticks out his foot and slams it down on the ground, stopping himself and his bike from completely toppling over.

Con "That was only five seconds!"

Josh "You made me lose my concentration by changing to 'monkey-kneebone!'"

Con "So?"

Josh "So—I like 'Mississippi!'"

Con "It shouldn't make any difference—I'm the one counting."

Josh "Yeah, well, it made me mess up. Let me do it again. But this time let's pick a counting word we both like."

Con "Okay. What about 'one smelly-fart, two smelly-fart...?'"

Josh "Or I know...'one snotty-nose, two snotty-nose...!'"

Josh and Con snort and chuckle at each other, proud of their made-up, time-keeping words.

Con "Forget balancing. I've got a
    better idea. Let's jump off a ramp!"
Josh "Yeah! Sick! But what ramp?"
Con "We'll make one. Come on."

The boys hop off their bikes and
charge around to Con's backyard.
They return with a plank of wood
and a couple of bricks. They make
their ramp—placing one end of the
wood on top of the two bricks.

Con "Okay. I'll go first."

Con stands up out of his bike seat and frantically crunches down on his pedals. He speeds toward the ramp as if he's an Olympic cyclist racing for the finishing line.

CHAPTER 3

Daredevils

Con makes it! He jumps off the ramp
and rides back to Josh.

Con "Did you see that? It was unreal! I felt like I was flying. I got about three feet off the ground."

Josh "No you didn't. It was only a few inches."

Con "No way! It was higher than that."

Josh "In your dreams. My turn. Here goes! *Ladies, gentlemen, and thrill-seekers, here comes the greatest stuntman in the world... the Amazing Josh!*"

Con "You're gonna jump a ramp, not make a rabbit disappear!"

Josh "Okay, then what should I call myself?"

Con "Nothing. Just jump!"

Josh "No, I have to have a name— like Evel Knievel!"

Con "Who?"

Josh "Evel Knievel! He was a
famous daredevil motorcycle rider
when my dad was young. He used
to jump over cars and stuff."

Con "Cool!"

Josh "So maybe I could be 'Evel
Josh'...nah, 'Jumping Josh'...or
'Jumping Josh Flash...'"

Con "How about 'Hurry Up Josh?'"

Josh "I got it! 'Jumping Josh
Warrior!'"

Con "That's it?"

Josh "Yeah! *And a sudden hush sweeps across the crowd as Jumping Josh Warrior prepares to take the leap of his life. Will he make it safely to the other side? No one has ever attempted to jump over a hundred cars before. This is going to be incredible...and here he goes!*"

Josh rushes toward the ramp and
sails over it easily. Con jumps again,
then so does Josh. Both boys
continue to ride over the ramp for
several minutes.

Con "This is boring. We've got to
jump over something that's real.
I know what!"

CHAPTER 4

Leap of Faith

Con rides his bike over to the side
fence. Josh wonders what Con has
in mind.

Josh "What are we gonna jump over?"
Con "You'll see. Chico! Here, Chico!"

Suddenly, an excited, little, white, fluffy dog appears out of nowhere and runs to Con.

Josh "You're not seriously going to jump over a dog?"

Con "Well, he's not *my* dog—he's the neighbor's."

Josh "But what if you miss?"

Con "I won't! Look how small he is."

Josh "Well I don't think *I* can jump over him."

Con "But you're the amazing Jumping Josh Warrior!"

Con hops off his bike and picks up Chico. He takes the dog and places him a few inches away from the end of the ramp.

Con "Stay, Chico! Don't move.
That's a good boy. Stay!"

Con runs back to Josh and hops
on his bike, ready to jump over his
neighbor's dog.

Josh "Poor little fella."

Con "He's gonna be okay! Just you wait and see. This is gonna be awesome—better than jumping over some fake cars.

And there's another hush from the crowd. They loved Jumping Josh Warrior, but now it's Captain Courageous Con's turn."

Josh "You mean, Captain *Crazy* Con!"

Con suddenly pedals as fast as he can toward the ramp, while Chico wags his tail, unaware of what is about to happen to him.

CHAPTER 5

Oh, No!

As the front tire of Con's bike makes
contact with the ramp, Josh
suddenly yells out.

Josh "Chico! Chico! Here, boy!"

Chico jumps up and scampers over to Josh, just as Con tries to leap over him. Josh lets out a huge sigh of relief and picks Chico up.

Con "What do you think you're doing? I would've made it!"

Josh "No, you wouldn't. Look! Your back wheel hit the ground right where Chico's head would've been."

Con "Really?"

Josh "Yeah—Chico would've ended up being a Chico pancake!"

Con "Phew! That was lucky."

Josh "Is there anything else we can jump over?"

Con "Um...wait, I know!"

Con hops off his bike and runs
into his house. He returns clutching
an armful of dolls.

Josh "Dolls?"

Con "Yeah, my sister's dumb dolls. We'll line them all up. And who cares if we miss and land on them, right?"

Josh "Cool!"

As Con and Josh prepare to leap
over the dolls, Con's sister suddenly
appears and yells, "Con!! Don't you
dare or I'm telling Mom!!"

Con "You ready to go for it,
  Jumping Josh Warrior?"

Josh "You bet, Captain Courageous
  Con!"

Both boys rush toward the ramp.
"MOM!!!!!!!!!!" screams Con's sister.

Con

BOYZ RULE!
Bike Lingo

Josh

axle The metal rod between the wheels that helps them to turn.

bike pump A tool used to pump up a flat tire.

helmet The thing that protects your head if you fall off your bike.

pedals What you put your feet on to push the bike.

puncture A hole your bike tire gets that makes the tire go flat.

Bike Musts

☞ Make sure you always put your helmet on before you ride your bike.

☞ Remember to check the air pressure in your tires.

☞ If you ride through puddles, make sure you wash the mud off your clothes before you go home.

☞ Learn how to fix tire punctures.

☞ Make sure that you know the road rules before you ride in the streets.

☞ If you want your bike to go faster, cut strips of cardboard and attach them to your wheel rims—the more wind you create in your spokes the more noise your bike will make and the faster it will go.

☞ Always wear shoes. If your feet hit the ground and you don't have shoes on, you might not have any feet left.

☞ If you're riding on a path in a park, make sure you ring your bell when you see someone else on the path.

☞ The most important bike rule is: look left, look right, then go ahead with extreme care.

BOYZ RULE!

Bike Instant Info

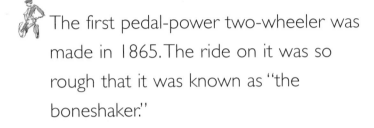 The first pedal-power two-wheeler was made in 1865. The ride on it was so rough that it was known as "the boneshaker."

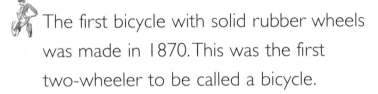 The first bicycle with solid rubber wheels was made in 1870. This was the first two-wheeler to be called a bicycle.

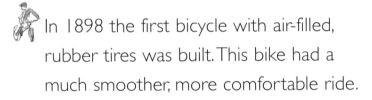 In 1898 the first bicycle with air-filled, rubber tires was built. This bike had a much smoother, more comfortable ride.

The first bicycle race took place in France, in 1868. The distance raced was 1.2 miles (2 kilometers).

BMX racing stands for bicycle motocross racing. In 1969, a group of kids in California who were fans of motocross (motorcycle races on dirt trails), organized the first BMX races.

 The most famous bike race in the world is the Tour de France. This race lasts for 21 days and is thousands of miles long.

 The highest bicycle bunny hop cleared a bar that was 3.9 feet (116 centimeters) high.

 The fastest bicycle speed ever recorded is 167 miles per hour (268.8 kilometers per hour). The bike was traveling behind a windshield.

 The longest bicycle ever built was 84 feet, 11 inches (25.9 meters) long.

 The best bicycle in the world is the one that you own.

Think Tank

1 What does Con try to jump over with his bike? What happens?

2 What do both Con and Josh want to try jumping over with their bikes?
What happens?

3 What side of the road do you ride on in the United States?

4 What is a tandem bike?

5 What is the most famous bike race in the world?

6 What do you think would have happened if Josh hadn't called Chico out of the way?

7 The story ends with Con's sister yelling for her mom so she can tell on the boys. What do you think happens next?

8 Why should you wear a helmet when you ride your bike?

Answers

1 Con tries to jump over the neighbor's dog, Chico, but Josh calls the dog to get him out of the way at the last minute.
2 Con and Josh want to try jumping over Con's sister's dolls, but his sister sees them, calls for her mom, and the book ends!
3 You ride on the right side of the street in the U.S.
4 A tandem is a bike for two people that has two seats and two sets of pedals.
5 The most famous bike race in the world is the Tour de France.
6 Answers will vary.
7 Answers will vary.
8 You should always wear a helmet when riding your bike because if you fall, it will protect your head.

How did you score?

- If you got most of the answers correct, then put on your bike helmet and go for a ride.

- If you got more than half of the answers correct, maybe you should only ride in the park.

- If you got less than half of the answers correct, either keep practicing or make sure you have a good pair of shoes for walking.

Felice →   ← Phil

Hi Guys!

We have lots of fun reading and want you to, too. We both believe that being a good reader is really important and so cool.

Try out our suggestions to help you have fun as you read.

At school, why don't you use "Bike Daredevils" as a play and you and your best friend can be the actors. Set the scene for your play. What props do you need? Maybe a bike helmet, or just use your imagination to pretend that you are at the park and about to have a bike race with your friends.

So...have you decided who is going to be Josh and who is going to be Con? Now, with your friends, read and act out our story in front of the class.

We have a lot of fun when we go to schools and read our stories. After we finish, the kids all clap really loudly. When you've finished your play your classmates will do the same. Just remember to look out the window—there might be a talent scout from a television station watching you!

Reading at home is really important and a lot of fun as well.

Take our books home and get someone in your family to read them with you. Maybe they can take on a part in the story.

Remember, reading is a whole lot of fun.

So, as the frog in the local pond would say, Read-it!

And remember, Boyz Rule!

Felice

BOYZ RULE!
When
We Were Kids

Phil

Phil "How did you make your bike go faster when you were a kid, Felice?"

Felice "I'd attach cardboard flaps to the rims of my back wheel."

Phil "And did that make you go faster?"

Felice "Well, you've heard of cars with big exhaust pipes, right?"

Phil "Yeah."

Felice "The louder the noise the faster the car goes. The same went for my bike…and it still does."

Phil "So, did that work?"

Felice "Yup, most of the time. But if that failed, I'd use my mouth, as I pedaled, to go *vrrrrrooooom!*"

BOYZ RULE!
What a Laugh!

Q Why can't a bike stand up?

A Because it's two-tired.